GU00949716

The Foundation St

ACKNOWLEDGEMENTS

Written by: Ros Bayley & Lynn Broadbent

Illustrated by: Peter Scott

Front Cover: Photograph of Tabatha & Dot
                  taken by Mac.

Produced by: Lynda Lawrence.

Published by: Lawrence Educational Publications
                  17 Redruth Road, Walsall,
                  West Midlands, WS5 3EJ

                  © Lawrence Educational 2003

ISBN: 1-903670-21-7

What is the Foundation Stage?

The Foundations Stage is a very important phase in children's lives .... a time when they especially need high quality care and education.

The aims of this distinct stage are to:
- give every 3, 4 and 5 year old the right to quality early years education.
- make it available in a wide range of different settings so that parents can choose the one that best meets their needs.
- help parents and early years educators work closely together to give children the best possible start in life.
- build on the education that children have already received at home.

The curriculum in the Foundation Stage is constructed to enable children to work towards and achieve the early learning goals. These goals are what most children are expected to achieve by the end of their time in a reception class. They are organised into areas of learning and involve:

- Personal, social and emotional development.
- Communication, language and literacy.
- Mathematical development.
- Knowledge and understanding of the world.
- Physical development.
- Creative development.

Why is the Foundation Stage important?

The Foundation Stage is based on comprehensive research about how young children learn, and will:

- recognise that children of this age learn differently from older children and adults;

- respect the young child's need to play and learn through first-hand experiences;

- teach children that they need to learn in the ways they most enjoy learning;

- introduce more formal teaching styles gradually and sensitively in order to keep children's interest in learning alive;

- ensure that all 3-5 year olds, including those with special educational needs, receive the same relevant quality curriculum;

- acknowledge that this is a time when children are forming attitudes about themselves and their ability to learn;

- help to ensure that children's early education equips them with the motivation to want to go on learning for the rest of their lives!

What difference will the Foundation Stage make to children?

The Foundation Stage will make a difference to children by:

- giving a greater emphasis to the development of communication skills which are so crucial to success in reading and writing;

- giving a clearer indication of their progress as they work towards achieving the early learning goals;

- providing a curriculum built around their need for frequent physical activity, with its benefit to their long term health and improved concentration skills;

- involving them in decisions about their learning through which they will develop initiative, confidence and self-reliance;

- helping to make sure that they will not be introduced to failure by being introduced to formal learning too early;

- putting a greater emphasis on the importance of their emotional well-being;

- making early education even more exciting and enjoyable for all children including those with special educational needs.

How can I help my child to learn?

Some of the things you can do that will really help your child to learn and progress well are to:

- listen carefully to what they have to say;
- involve yourself in their play;
- make time to talk about things that are important to them;
- share books, songs and stories;
- count numbers in everyday situations;
- when out and about, notice signs, colours, shapes, buildings etc.
- focus on their strengths and encourage and praise their efforts;
- encourage their independent skills;
- help them to understand that learning sometimes involves getting things wrong;
- understand their need to play and learn through first-hand experiences;
- understand that they don't always want to talk about what they have done at school, and that even if they do, they will only tell you the bits they want you to know!
- realise that when you are 3, 4 or 5 a full day at your setting is hard work;
- avoid putting them under too much pressure, allow time for relaxation;
- work closely with your child's setting and share information about your child with the staff.

Introduction

The activities that follow are organised into areas of learning, but it is important to remember that as you try them out you will be helping your child in a whole variety of ways and enriching their all round learning.

Within the range of this publication we can only suggest a limited number of activities, but we are sure that as you explore them you will think of many, many more!

By supporting your child in this way, you will be really helping them at what is probably the most important time in their lives, and hopefully you'll have lots of fun too!

Ros Bayley

Notes

Knowledge and Understanding of the World

This area of learning is all about making sense of the world in a way that will lay foundations for later work in science, history, geography, design technology and information, and communication technology. Young children with their natural curiosity and drive to make sense of the world will enjoy exploring the following experiences with you.

Scavenger Hunt

What you need:
Containers or boxes in which the children can store their collections.

What you do:
Make a list of all the things that you are going to hunt for. What you put on the list will depend on where you are at the time, e.g. the garden, the park, in the house or at the seaside etc.

Your list may look something like this:

1. A leaf
2. A stone
3. Something red
4. Something prickly
5. A flower
6. A stick
7. A coin
8. Something made of plastic
9. Something soft
10. Something you use to eat your dinner

Happy Hunting!

How you will have helped your child:

- As you read from the list you will be demonstrating to your child that print conveys meaning.

- As you talk about the things you find you will extend your child's knowledge and vocabulary.

- As you sort the items out you will help your child to develop important classification skills.

- When you count the items to see how many things you have found you will be developing counting and number skills.

You can play this game lots of times with different lists.

Painters and Decorators

What you will need:
Large paint brushes, old rolls of wallpaper, bucket of paste, scissors and some cardboard boxes.

What you do:
This is a great activity for doing outside when the weather is fine.

Let your child help you mix the paste, and talk with them about how much water is needed and what the paste looks and feels like. Then let them cut up the wallpaper and 'paper' the cardboard boxes.

Use the large paintbrushes with plain water and 'paint' walls, sheds and buildings. Talk with them about how long this paint will take to dry.

Write their name on the wall with water and encourage them to have a go at writing it themselves. See how long it takes to disappear.

How you will have helped your child:

- Mixing the paste will encourage your child to think twice about texture and consistency, and learn new words to describe what they see and feel.

- Cutting up the wallpaper will develop your child's hand/eye co-ordination and help them to understand about measuring.

- Painting the walls with water will help your child to think about where the 'writing' has gone and begin to understand about evaporation.

13

Sound Games

What you need:
A blindfold and a variety of household objects that make a noise, e.g. keys, kitchen timer, spoons, saucepans, mobile phone, squeaky toy etc.

What you do:
Let your child explore the collection of objects. Encourage them to talk about and describe the different sounds that they make, then use the blindfold to play a listening game to see if the children can identify which object made the sound.

Swap roles with your child so that you are wearing the blindfold and doing the guessing, and they are choosing what sound to make.

How you will have helped your child:

- As you play this game you will develop your child's ability to discriminate between sounds, and this is very important in helping them gain some of the important skills necessary for reading.

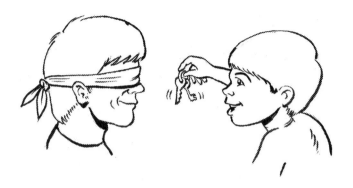

- You will also be developing your child's listening skills and this is very beneficial as listening is such an important part of learning.

The Potato Run

What you need:
A potato, a shoe box and some strips of card.

What to do:
Cut a hole about the size of a ten pence piece in one end of the box, then tie the strips of card and position them about 3-4 cms apart to make a channel. It's more fun if you zig-zag the channel to make it move like a maze.

Now place the potato in the box at the opposite end to the hole and put the lid on the box.

Check the potato every few days to see how far the shoots have grown towards the light.

Encourage your child to look closely at the shoots and help them to describe what is happening.

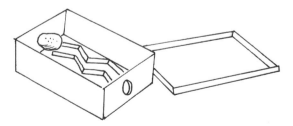

How you will have helped your child:

- As you observe the growth of the shoots and talk about what is happening you will be helping your child to express their ideas and notice change.

- If you encourage them to think about whether the shoots will reach the hole and how long it will take, you will be developing their ability to predict.

- Time spent talking about why the shoot is behaving in the way it is will really help your child to understand that light is necessary for growth.

- Growing things will also help your child to begin to develop an understanding of time.

Change The Colour

What you need:
Glass jars, food colouring, sticks of celery or some white carnations.

What to do:
Get your child to mix a teaspoonful of food colouring with some water and then place a carnation or freshly cut stick of celery into the jar. After a few hours the capillary action will have worked enough for you to see the dye being taken up the stem.

Encourage your child to offer explanations for what is happening.
Try adding some plastic or silk flowers and talk about why they haven't taken up the water!

How you will have helped your child:

- As you draw their attention to what is happening, listen carefully to what they say and talk about what is happening, you will be extending their vocabulary and helping them to share their ideas.

- When you talk about how long it has taken for the celery or the flower to take up the water you will be developing their ideas about time.

- If you add some plastic flowers you will help your child to recognise and talk about differences and make comparisons.

Lay A Trail

What you need:
A small parcel and some slices of bread.

What you do:
Wrap a small but interesting item up, e.g. a packet of Smarties or a small toy and hide it somewhere in the garden or the house. If you are doing this activity in the house you may prefer to use pieces of paper rather than bread.

Lay a trail of small pieces of bread from the door to the parcel and wait and see if the children notice it. If they don't, (which is unlikely!) draw their attention to it. Talk about the route you are taking as you follow the trail, e.g. round the corner, through the alleyway, behind the bushes etc.

When the parcel is finally discovered express your surprise and enjoy opening it with the children. Talk about how it got there and who might have laid the trail.

How you will have helped your child:

- As you encourage them to think about who laid the trail and left the surprise, you will be stimulating and extending your child's imagination.

- When you talk about the route taken to the surprise you will be helping your child to learn new words and develop early geographical concepts.

Notes

Creative Development

Creativity is a process that is important to so many things in life, and the more we can do to develop children's creativity at this crucial stage, the more we advantage the children. This area of learning covers art, music, dance, role-play and imaginative play, but it is important to remember that creativity is possible in just about any area of life. Some people are creative in the kitchen, some in the garden and some with DIY. Wherever you express your creativity, your child will gain hugely from sharing that process with you.

Weaving on a grand scale

What you need:
Pea netting, (or a large piece of trellis) strips of fabric, ribbon, wool etc

What you do:
Suspend a large piece of plastic netting on a wall, between two trees or peg to the ground with tent pegs. If you already have some trellis work in the garden you can simply make use of that! Show your child how to weave the fabric through the netting, talking them through the process as you do so. Once you have done this they will be able to experiment with different materials and create a variety of effects.

You may also like to experiment with weaving onto a variety of frames e.g. Bend wire coat hangers into different shapes and use as a basis for weaving. Lash some branches together and weave fabric though the intertwined twigs or make a pyramid out of garden canes. Encourage your child to think about good places in which to display their completed wall hangings, mobiles or structures. Their ideas about this may be different to yours and a degree of compromise may be called for!

How you will have helped your child:

- The intricate process of weaving will help to develop their co-ordination.

- Talking about what they are doing as they weave will develop their language skills and vocabulary.

- Thinking about which materials they will use will help them to make choices and decisions.

- Making structures from different materials will help your child to solve problems.

- This activity will provide your child with a way of expressing their creativity.

Make a Scarecrow

What you need:
A broom handle, some old clothes, bits and pieces for making features and some straw or hay.

What you do:
This is a great activity to do if you have just planted some seeds in the garden.

Talk to your child about what they would like the scarecrow to look like and if you can find any pictures of scarecrows in books, talk about the pictures and encourage your child to express their opinions about which features they like and dislike.

Once you have made the scarecrow together try to think of a good name for him, (or her!) You might try extending your child's imagination by suggesting that the scarecrow comes to life at night. Get them to think about some of the things they think he might like to do!

How you will have helped your child:

- If as part of this activity you searched for books about scarecrows, you will have helped your child to understand about the ways in which we can find things out from books.

- As you talked through the process of making the scarecrow you will have extended your child's vocabulary.

- As you talked with your child about other possible ways of scaring the birds away you will have extended their thinking skills and encouraged them to think in a problem solving way.

- The experience of making the scarecrow will have involved them in estimating and measuring and given them experience of the various ways in which things can be joined together.

Stone Painting

What you need:
Some nice flat stones and some suitable paint, glue, shells sequins etc. Some soapy water for washing the stones.

What you do:
Start by going on a stone hunt. As you do this you will probably find all manner of interesting things! e.g. Spiders, bugs, worms and beetles. Take time to talk with your child about these things.

Once you have found some suitable stones wash them in the soapy water. Talk to your child about what is happening to the stones and how they are changing as they get wet. Some children get so interested in washing the stones and watching them dry that they don't get round to the decorating bit straight away!

Once they have finished exploring the stones in the water support them to select from the available materials and decorate the stones. Encourage them to think about other things that could be used to decorate the stones.

How you will have helped your child:

- You will have extended their knowledge and understanding of the world as you searched for the stones, talked about them and discussed the places in which you found them and the things you found close to them.

- This process will also have extended their language skills and helped them to learn new words.

- As they compare the number and size of the stones they have collected you will be encouraging important mathematical learning.

- As they wash the stones and observe the way in which they change they will be engaged in scientific learning.

- As they decorate the stones their creativity and imagination will be stimulated

Cardboard Boxes

What you need:
A selection of cardboard boxes with holes cut in the sides and top so that your child can 'wear' them.

What you do:
Encourage your child to think about all the different ways in which they could use the boxes, e.g. robots, cars, tractors, monsters etc. Let them use their voices to make sound effects! Get them to think about other ways in which they could use the boxes and add some old bed sheets so that they can build dens.

Open the ends of the boxes and join several boxes together with parcel tape to make a tunnel. You'll be amazed at just how much you can do with some old cardboard boxes!

How you will have helped your child:

- As they play with the boxes and talk with you about what they are doing they will learn and practise positional language, e.g. through, inside, outside, under, over, around, across etc.

- As you and your child talk about what the boxes could be used for you will stimulate their imagination and help them to think creatively.

- If you use more than one box you will help them to practise joining skills.

- By encouraging your child to use sound effects you will be helping them to explore sounds and this is very important for later reading development.

What am I doing?

What you need:
No resources required.

What you do:
Perform a simple mime for your child, e.g. washing your face, eating a banana, driving a car or brushing your teeth. Encourage them to guess what you are doing and copy your mime.

Once they have got the idea of the game let them take the lead so that you can try and guess what they are doing and copy their mime.

As an extension of this game, make a collection of simple household objects, e.g. a sweeping brush, a wooden spoon a saucepan or a plastic plate and carry out a mime using one of the objects for something other than its intended purpose e.g. the plastic plate could become a steering wheel or the wooden spoon a lollipop.

Once again, as soon as your child has got the idea of the game you can reverse roles.

How you will have helped your child:

- This activity will help your child to concentrate and observe. It will also extend their imagination.

- Once you reverse roles you will be helping your child to think creatively.

- As you play this game you will help them to understand the way in which mime can be used as a form of communication and how one thing can be used to represent another.

Listen and Find

What you need:
Some bells or whistles or other household objects that make a noise e.g. an old saucepan and a wooden spoon with which to beat it.

What you do:
Show your child the 'instruments' that are to be used for this activity and explain that they need to cover their eyes while you hide and play one of the instruments. Tell them that when they hear the sound they have got to follow the sound and try to find you. Once they understand the game you can reverse roles.

How you will have helped your child:

- As you play this game you will be helping them to explore sounds. If you also talk about the sounds that you are making you will extend their vocabulary e.g.: loud, soft, quiet, near, far, close etc.

- As you play this game you will help your child to understand why games have to have rules to make them work.

- As you change roles you will support them in taking turns.

- You will be helping them to enjoy themselves and to experience the excitement of playing games.

Notes

Physical Development

The more we learn about how the brain works, the more we realise that movement is essential to learning, and this area of learning is all about children developing confidence and control of the way they move and work with tools and equipment. Before children can gain mastery of the fine movements needed for such things as writing, they must first gain mastery of large movements. The activities given here, and others like them, will help them to do just that

Take Aim!

What You Need:
Skittles, (these can be made using plastic bottles weighted with a little water) buckets of water, sponges and other assorted items with which the children can take aim.
Suitable protective clothing.

What you do:
Set up a series of targets and let your child take pot shots at them with sponges that have been soaked in the buckets of water.

If you want to develop this activity further, number the skittles and other targets and have paper and pencil ready for recording the score.

Talk with your child about which things are easiest to knock over and which things are more difficult. Encourage them to give reasons why they think the way they do.

See if they can think of anything else that could be used as a target. They usually can!

How you will have helped your child:

- As they take aim at the targets your child will develop their hand/eye co-ordination.

- Throwing the sponges will help develop their strength and physical dexterity.

- Aiming at the targets will help your child to think about and learn about forces.

- Counting how many things they have knocked down and keeping score will help their mathematical development.

- If they play this game with you or with other children they will learn about taking turns.

Snowball Fight

What you need:
A pile of newspaper and a roll of sellotape.

What you do:
Show your child how to make 'snowballs' by crumpling up the sheets of newspaper and securing them with sellotape.

Once they have accumulated enough snowballs you can set groundrules and the snowball fight can begin.

Ask them to think about where would be the best place for a snowball fight and if there is anything that needs to happen in order to make sure that no-one gets hurt. For example, not aiming the snowballs at people's faces.

Talk with them about what kind of rules are needed to make the game work well.

How you will have helped your child:

Playing this game will help to develop their hand/eye co-ordination, strength and dexterity, and these things are very important because they are a basis for later work in reading and writing.

Making up rules for the game will help to develop important social skills and ideas about fairness.

If you decide you want to keep a score you will be helping to develop number skills.

Playing this game will also help to develop positional language e.g. Close, high, low, above, far, near, etc

Flashlight Fun

What you need:
Some torches, large cardboard boxes, a garden table and some sheets or blankets.

What you do:
Use a large cardboard box to make a dark hidey-hole. If you don't have a large box, drape blankets over a garden table or a clothes horse. Once inside, let your child explore the space with a torch. Talk about what it feels like inside the box and see if they can think of anything they could put over the torch to change the colour of the light, e.g. some coloured paper.

Join several boxes together with parcel tape to make a long dark tunnel and let them crawl through the tunnel, lighting their way with the torch. If they are playing this game with friends they can see how many children will fit into the dark space.

If you have any 'scary stories,' read or tell them inside the hide-hole in the torchlight.

How you will have helped your child:

- Making the dark hidey-hole and joining the boxes together will help to develop their physical dexterity.

- Exploring the dark space with the torch will help to develop scientific ideas about dark and light and will also extend their vocabulary.

- Spending time in the dark hidey-hole or the dark tunnel will stimulate your child's imagination.

Balloon Hockey

What you need:
Some balloons, plastic bottles and some suitable music (optional!).

What you do:
Make a simple goal using two markers and then release several balloons into the space available. The object of this game is for your child to use the plastic bottles to propel the balloons into the goal. In fact, you don't even have to have a goal as they may simply enjoy moving the balloons around the space! If you do this activity to music the type of music used will greatly influence the activity, so don't make it TOO exciting!

How you will have helped your child:

- Propelling the balloons with the plastic bottle will really help to develop hand/eye coordination.

- Using music with this activity will help to develop your child's imagination.

- When you talk about what is happening to the balloons you will be developing positional language and helping your child to learn new vocabulary.

- If you keep a tally of how many balloons go through the goal you will be developing counting skills.

The Obstacle Course

What you need:
Chairs, cardboard boxes, sheets or blankets and other objects that can be used as obstacles.

What you do:
This game can be played inside or out, but is probably better played outside. Using the things available construct an obstacle course. Open up the ends of cardboard boxes to make tunnels, construct low hurdles that can be jumped over and use stones as markers to denote the direction of the course. Make pathways using tape or string and cut up pieces of card to make stepping stones. Use leaves, branches and twigs as obstacles to go over, under or through. Suspend a broom over two upturned buckets to make an obstacle to 'limbo' under! Use arrow or numbers to show the direction of the course. If you have a ladder or some boards, lay these flat on the ground or at a slightly raised angle for your child to balance along.

How you will have helped your child:

- Playing on the obstacle course will help your child to develop strength, balance and physical dexterity.

- As you talk them through the obstacle course they will learn positional language i.e. over, under, through, around, high, low etc.

- As they navigate their way around the course they will learn about sequence, order and number.

- If you encourage them to think about other ways of creating obstacles you will be developing their imagination and helping them to think creatively.

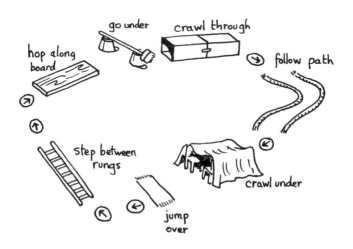

Pasta Mobiles

What you need:
Some wire coat hangers, string or thread, pasta tubes and some spray paint.

What you do:
Talk with your child about what shape they would like their mobile to be and then bend the wire coat hanger into the required shape. Show them how to thread the pasta tubes onto the string and tie them to the coat hanger. When they have finished threading the strings of pasta, take them outside and let your child paint their completed mobile.

Discuss with them where they think the mobile would look nice, and once dry, display the finished piece of work. Observe the mobile to see how much it is moving and see if your child can think of ways in which you could make it move even more.

Ask them if they can think of other things that could be hung on the mobile and offer your own suggestions e.g. buttons, feathers, pieces of foil etc. See if they can suggest other uses for the pasta tubes e.g. to make necklaces or pictures.

How you will have helped your child:

- Threading the pasta onto the string will help your child to develop fine muscle control.

- Making the mobiles will help to develop their imagination and creativity.

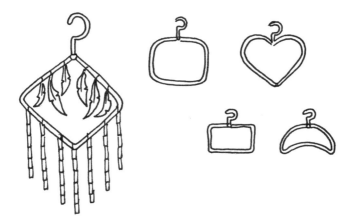

- Observing the mobiles and thinking of ways to make them move will help to develop early scientific concepts.

Notes

Mathematical Development

This area of learning involves children in counting, sorting, matching, pattern making and working with numbers, shapes and measures, and when this learning is embedded in simple everyday activities it has great meaning for the young child. The activities that follow should enable such learning to take place in a context where they can have fun and enjoy themselves and build confidence in dealing with mathematical ideas.

51

Number Hunt

What you need:
Numbers written on pieces of card or cut from boxes and packaging. Plastic, wooden or magnetic numbers if you have any of these. A box or bag to collect the numbers in.

What you do:
Before your child gets up or while they are doing something else, hide the numbers around the house and outside. Hide them under stones, hang them from trees, place them behind things and leave them on the grass.

Explain to your child that the object of the game is for them to find as many numbers as they can. Talk with them about where they think the numbers may be hidden.

Once they have found all the numbers encourage them to sort them out and see whether there are more of some than others.

Reverse roles, and let your child hide the numbers for you to find! You can also play this game with shapes, objects, letters and words.

How you will have helped your child:

- As they find and identify the numbers you will be helping them to recognise numbers.

- As they search for the numbers you will be helping them to learn positional language.

- As they count how many numbers they have collected you will be helping them to develop counting skills.

- As they look to see which numbers they have most of you will be helping them to learn how to compare amounts.

- As they hide the numbers for you they will develop their creative thinking.

Wrap up some presents

What you need:
A collection of different sized boxes and some things to put inside (some that are heavy and some that are lighter).

What you do:
Wrap up the presents and encourage your child to offer their ideas about what they think might be inside the boxes. Encourage them to give reasons for their guesses. Make sure that some of the larger boxes have something very light inside and that some of the smaller boxes contain something heavy! Once your child understands the game let them place some objects inside the boxes so that you can guess what is inside. Help them to wrap the presents up.

How you will have helped your child:

- As they guess what is inside the presents you will develop their logical and creative thinking and help them to understand the concepts of heavy and light.

- As they wrap up the presents for you they will learn more about estimating and measuring.

- Throughout this activity they will develop language skills and learn new vocabulary.

Hunt the Thimble

What you need:
A suitable object for hiding.

What you do:
This age old game is excellent for helping your child to learn positional language. Simply ask them to hide their eyes or go out of the room while you hide the selected object. Once it is hidden they can search for it while you give them guidance by saying 'warmer' or 'colder.' Once they get the hang of the game they can hide an object for you and give you guidance as you search for it.

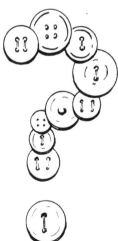

How you will have helped your child:

- As already mentioned, they will learn more about the language of position.

- As they give you guidance to help you find the hidden object they will develop their concentration skills.

- Thinking of good places to hide the object will develop their creative thinking.

The Button Box

What you need:
An old box or tin and a collection of old buttons. It may take you a while to make this collection but it is well worth it!

What you do:
Once your child knows that you have such a collection they will probably be keen to play with it, especially if it contains some large, sparkly, unusual buttons!

Tip the buttons out onto a tray or other suitable surface and watch what your child does with them. Without much encouragement children are generally keen to sort, match, count and make patterns with the buttons. If you can get hold of a few badges and medals this will make the activity even more interesting!

Talk with your child about what they are doing and encourage them to think about where the buttons, badges and medals might have come from.

How you will have helped your child:

• As previously mentioned, this activity will provide opportunities for your child to sort, match, count, compare and make patterns.

• As they think about where the things might have come from they will develop their imagination.

• Talking about the buttons and where they might have come from will help them to learn new vocabulary.

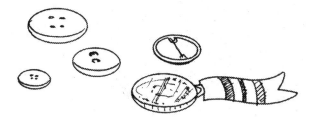

• If you include some buttons from some of their old clothes you will be helping them to remember and think about time concepts.

• You can also do this activity with collections of lids, boxes, pebbles, shells etc.

The Tray Game

What you need:
A tray with a collection of objects and a piece of cloth or a tea towel.

What you do:
This one is an old favorite!
Place a variety of objects onto a tray. Explain to your child that they will have a little while to study the objects and that the idea of the game is to try to remember the things that they can see on the tray. Then cover the tray with the cloth and see how many items they can remember.

How you will have helped your child:

- Playing this game will help your child to develop the skill of visualisation, and this is very important for later work in mathematics.

- As they try to remember the items on the tray they will develop concentration and memory skills.

- If you put some unusual items on the tray you will stimulate your child's curiosity and help them to learn new vocabulary.

Fun with smarties

What you need:
One packet of smarties, or similar.

What you do:
Lay the smarties out on a suitable surface and encourage your child to sort and count them. Lay some of them out in a line (maybe five or six) and get your child to study the line and try to remember the sequence of the smarties. Then get them to close their eyes while you remove one of the smarties. See if they can identify the colour of the missing smartie.

Line the smarties up and see how many there are of each colour. Make comparisons e.g. are there more red ones than orange ones?

Line all the smarties up in a long line to see how far they will stretch.

Encourage your child to guess how long the line will be before they begin.

Try similar things with wine gums, jelly babies etc. You'll be amazed at how much mathematical development you can promote with a packet of sweets!

How you will have helped your child:

- As they play with the sweets in this way your child will be sorting, matching, counting and comparing.

- Trying to remember which sweet is missing will help your child to develop their ability to concentrate, visualise and remember.

- Guessing how far a line of smarties will stretch will help your child develop the ability to estimate.

Notes

Communication, Language and Literacy

This area of learning is about speaking and listening and developing the important oral language skills so crucial to later work in reading and writing. It also involves reading a range of simple texts and writing for a range of purposes. Engaging in the following activities will help your child to see literacy as something important and desirable.

Treasure Hunt

What you need:
Some 'treasure' and a series of letters giving information about where it is hidden.

What you do:
Post a letter to your child saying that if they follow the clues it will lead them to some treasure! This could be some special sweets, a toy, a cuddly toy in a box or anything else that your child would enjoy discovering.

The first letter could say something like: Go to the tree at the end of the garden and you will find an envelope tied to the branch of the apple tree.

The next letter might say: Look under the large stone by the shed and you will find a message.

Continue until the treasure is found.

Once your child understands the process they can help you to lay a treasure hunt for someone else.

How you will have helped your child:

- As they follow the directions received in the letter they will extend their understanding of the ways in which text conveys meaning.

- As they search for the clues they will extend their vocabulary and learn positional language.

- As they think about what the treasure may be and who put it in it's hiding place they will extend their imagination.

- If they lay a trail for someone else they will engage in creative thinking.

Bookmaking

What you need:
Some paper, felt pens, crayons, old magazines, postcards, etc. and a camera if one is available.

What you do:
Making books about things which are of interest to them is an excellent way of getting children interested in text, and if they are the star and the main character in the book then they will want to read it again and again! Once you and your child have identified a focus for your book, enjoy cutting, sticking, drawing and captioning with your child. Encourage them to make decisions about what should go on each page and what the text should say. Accept their ideas and try not to impose too many of your own ideas. (This is much harder than it seems!)

Some possible subjects for books might be:
>   All about my holidays.
>   My favourite stories
>   My family and friends
>   My favourite food
>   The things I like to do
>   My alphabet book
>   My book of favourite rhymes and songs.
>   My recipe book
>   My address book
>   My favourite TV programmes

How you will have helped your child:

Book making is a powerful way of helping children understand that text and books convey meaning.

• As your child makes books they will extend their vocabulary and communicate their thoughts and feelings in a meaningful way.

• Book making will provide your child with the opportunity to see an adult writing and engage in mark making for themselves.

• Bookmaking will provide your child with the opportunity to organise, sequence and clarify their thinking.

• Making books with you will stimulate your child's creativity and imagination.

Post a pet toy

What you need:
A small soft toy that will capture your child's imagination.

What you do:
Wrap the toy up and send it through the post to your child. You could include a list of instructions for how it should be looked after, or a letter from 'the person who sent it,' explaining why they have done so.

Then:
- Help your child write back to the person who sent it.

- Help the pet to write a postcard home, (persuade someone to reply to the postcard, or do it yourself, the correspondence can then go on indefinitely!)

- Write a book about your pet's adventures.

How you will have helped your child:

- This activity will help to develop your child's creativity and imagination.

- Writing about your pet will provide your child with a valuable opportunity to watch an adult writing and learn about the writing process, and this is very important as young children learn by listening and watching!

- Talking about the process will help to develop your child's vocabulary.

- Posting and receiving parcels and postcards will help your child learn about the ways in which people communicate

Favourite Food

What you need:
For this activity you will need to collect boxes and wrappers from favourite food. For example, chocolate bar wrappers, crisp packets, biscuit wrappers etc.

What you do:
Explain to your child that you are going to cut out words and letters from the wrappers and packaging to make a shopping list, poster or message.

Talk with them about the various forms of print and text. You will be amazed at what they notice. In fact, they frequently notice subtleties that adults aren't even aware of.

If you decide to make a shopping list, take it with you and use it when you go shopping and this will give the activity real meaning!

How you will have helped your child:

- Exploring the packaging will help your child to learn more about the printed word.

- Using the shopping list will help your child to understand about the way in which we can use text to help us to organise our lives.

- Talking about their favourite foods will enable them to express their opinions and preferences and extend their vocabulary.

The Message Board

What you need:
A cork notice board or wipeable whiteboard and some pens and markers.

What you do:
This is an ongoing activity that is excellent for demonstrating the way in which we use writing to organise our lives.

If your child tells you that you have forgotten to do something that you said you would, you can immediately write a note on the message board to remind yourself of what you need to do! If they identify something that you need to buy from the shops you can put a reminder on the board. If you are looking forward to someone's birthday you can write reminders about cards and presents. If there is something your child needs to remember you can help them to put a message on the message board.

How you will help your child:

- Through this ongoing use of the message board your child will begin to understand the importance of the written word in daily life.

- They will have valuable opportunities to see an adult writing for a real purpose.

- As they think about past, present and future events featured on the notice board you will be helping them with the development of time concepts.

The Bag of Tricks

What you need:
A selection of interesting objects (probably about five or six) and a feely bag. The objects could be things like a map, some binoculars, a crystal, a key, a gold coin, a piece of rope, a silk handkerchief etc.

What you do:
Place the items into the feely bag and explain that you are going to make up a story using the contents of the bag.

Set the scene by encouraging your child to think of a setting for the story and then begin by saying: 'One day when we were at the….........we found a...........' (your child selects something from the bag). Then continue.........……..' we decided to............' (what you decide will very much depend on what is selected from the bag). 'After that we...........'(another item is chosen) "Then we................'(your child chooses again) "In the end.......……....'
Keep selecting items until the story feels complete, then recall your story, changing any bits you are not happy with.

How you will help your child:

- Making up a story of this sort will really help to develop your child's language skills.

- As they work on the story their creativity and imagination will be stimulated.

- Recalling the story will develop their sense of time, order, sequence and logic.

- They will increase their sense of story and begin to see themselves as storytellers.

Notes

Personal, Social and Emotional Development

This important area of learning is all about helping your child to learn about themselves and their place in the family, the community and the wider world.

They will begin to recognise, acknowledge and understand about feelings and begin to understand what is right, what is wrong, and why. By a gradual process they will learn that people have different needs, views, cultures and beliefs that need to be treated with respect. They will also learn that they deserve respect from others.

This area of learning will involve your child in learning how to take turns, operate as part of a group and build relationships. As they carry out activities in this and the other areas of learning they will gain in confidence and independence and develop a love of learning.

79

I can do it by myself!

What you need:
A colourful A4 book.

What you do:
Every time your child does something all by themselves, celebrate the occasion by recording their achievements in their 'I can do it by myself book.' Encourage them to comment on how they feel about what they have achieved and record their comments in the book. Draw pictures with them and for them and maybe add a photograph or two!

Some of the things that you may like to record are e.g. riding a bike, buttoning a coat, tying their own laces etc.

How you will have helped your child:

- Focusing on their achievements and recording them will really help them to see themselves as capable people who are able to take care of their own needs and learn to do new things.

- As they watch you write in their book they will see writing used for a real purpose.

- When you look back through the book at all the things they have learned you will help to develop their concept of time.

Helping Out

What you need:
This will vary according to the situation.

What you do:
In order that your child can have the opportunity to learn about the importance of helping others, why not identify a charity that they can support in some way. The charity that you select will probably depend on the sorts of things your child is interested in but could be something like adopting a whale, a gorilla or a dog. Alternatively, there are now many opportunities to support children through charities like Oxfam and Action Aid.

The advantage of these schemes is that your child will receive regular information about the animal or the children they are supporting, but if this is not viable there are many other ways of helping out. Why not get them to turn out the toys that they have outgrown and donate them to the charity shop or save some pennies for a charity of their choice.

How you will have helped your child:

- Even very young children need to feel that they can make a difference and by facilitating them to help someone else you will be developing their sense of empathy and social responsibility.

- Through thinking about others your child will build on their awareness of the wider world and the needs of others.

Do you remember when?

What you need:
A selection of photographs showing things that you have done together, e.g. places you have visited, parties you have held or been to etc.

What you do:
Select some interesting photographs taken over time and see what your child remembers about those occasions. As you look at the photographs talk with your child about how they make you feel and help them to express their feelings.

Listen carefully to what they have to say and answer their questions as they arise. Slip in some photographs of yourself and members of your family that were taken before your child was born and see what they have to say about these. They will very often ask where they were!

How you will have helped your child:

- As you remember a range of events and talk about how you and your child feel about these times you will be developing their vocabulary of 'feelings' words.

- This activity will also help to develop your child's concept of time.

- As they review the collection of photographs your child will enhance their understanding of how they fit into a family, a community and the wider world.

My Book of Feelings

What you need:
An A4 book or scrapbook

What you do:
Make a list of feelings that are commonly experienced by a young child. For example, happy, scared, disappointed, sorry, hopeful, irritable, sad, angry, embarrassed etc.

Collect photographs and pictures of people who look as if they may be feeling these things. Talk with your child about the things that cause them to feel these things and share your own experiences with them.

Discuss the ways in which people express emotions to help your child to see that some forms of expression are better and less hurtful than others.

Share stories with them and talk about the feelings of the characters in the story.

How you will have helped your child:

- As you talk about the range of feelings experienced by human beings you will be helping your child to learn about emotions and what it means to be human.

- As you talk with them about your own feelings you will be helping them to understand that everyone feels the whole range of emotions.

- Through this process you will help your child to talk about feelings and build their feelings vocabulary.

Plan an Event

What you need:
A reason to celebrate and pen and paper for planning.

What you do:
Once you have identified a reason for a celebration, take your pen and paper so that you and your child can begin planning. Decide who will be invited, when and where the event will take place and what will be needed. This will provide your child with an opportunity to think about the people who are important to them and a context through which they can show their feelings.

Make invitations, plan menus and go shopping for all the things you will need, then make your preparations, look forward to the event and have fun!

Make sure that you involve your child throughout the whole process so that they feel that they really have been instrumental in making the event happen.

How you will have helped your child:

• Planning an event in this way will provide your child with a real context in which they can experience the joy of giving something to the people who are important to them.

• Through this activity they will be able to experience what it feels like to make choices and decisions

• They will learn about what is involved in planning an event and gain experience in thinking ahead.

Recycle, recycle, recycle!

What you need:
Old clothes, newspaper, bottles or cans etc.

What you do:
This may seem terribly obvious, but the simple act of recycling can provide your child with some really valuable learning opportunities.

Set them the task of collecting and counting bottles or newspapers and take them to the places where they can recycle their collection. Talk with them about what happens to such things when they are not recycled and begin to help them to think about how this will affect the environment.

Encourage them to keep a tally of the amounts that they have recycled and set targets for what they think they can achieve.

How you will have helped your child:

- The simple act of recycling will help your child to understand the importance of caring for the environment and enable them to see that they have, albeit in a small way, the ability to make a difference.

- Organising and counting the collection will help to develop their logic and number skills.

- Talking about the environment will help your child develop personal and social responsibility.

Notes